Wizards

Christopher Rawson
Adapted by Gill Harvey

Illustrated by
Stephen Cartwright

Reading Consultant: Alison Kelly
Roehampton University of Surrey

Contents

Chapter 1

Long, long ago

Long ago, lots of people believed in wizards. They thought there were good ones, who helped people...

...and bad ones, who cast evil spells.

They thought there were old wizards, with long white beards...

...and young ones, who were still learning their magic tricks.

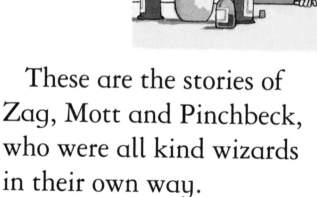

These are the stories of Zag, Mott and Pinchbeck, who were all kind wizards in their own way.

4

Chapter 2

The mean man

Zag was a wonderful wizard. He looked after children who had nowhere else to live. The children adored him.

But Zag was so busy caring for the children that he didn't do any magic. In fact, he forgot his spells. Until, one day...

Look! Not even a button.

"We don't have any money left," he said sadly.

"What are we going to do?" asked Tom, one of the boys.

"Don't worry!" said Zag. "I know how we can make some money."

I'll teach you some tricks.

The children were excited. Did Zag mean magic tricks?

But Zag didn't teach the children magic. First, he taught them how to juggle.

Then he taught them clever jumping tricks, and acrobatics.

Finally, the children put on a show for the villagers. It was a great success! Everyone laughed and clapped and gave the children money.

Bravo!

Well, almost everyone.

One man walked past, muttering to himself. He didn't give them any money — even though he had bags of gold.

His name was Mervin the Miser and it suited him.

He was a miser – as mean as his name.

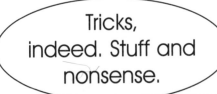

Mervin stomped off to his house before anyone could spot him. Safe inside, he shut the door with a bang.

The money from the show didn't last. By Christmas Eve, it had run out completely. Outside, it snowed. Inside, the children's tummies grumbled.

And Zag had run out of ideas. "I'm sorry, children," he said. "Maybe we should all just go to bed."

Zag was very old and tired. The children knew he'd done his best.

But they didn't give up.
"Let's go to Zag's Secret
Room," they whispered.

"Maybe we'll find a magic
spell to help us."

The children crept into the
room. Zag hadn't used any
spells for a long, long time.
The room was covered in dust
and cobwebs.

Oooo...
it's spooky
in here...

Jack, one of the older boys, found a rusty can. "Laughing powder!" he whispered. "Do you think it works?"

There was only one way to find out...

The children slipped out of the wizard's house and into the snowy night. They headed for Mervin the Miser's house.

Mervin was fast asleep.
Jack tiptoed to his bed, and
sprinkled laughing powder
all over him.

Mervin didn't stir. He just
grunted in his sleep.

Then Alice pulled a feather from the pillow. She reached for Mervin's toes...

...and tickled them. Mervin woke up at once! The children jumped back, afraid.

"Ha ha!" cried Mervin, with a huge smile. He started to laugh. He laughed until the tears rolled down his cheeks.

"HA! HA! Stop!" he begged. "I haven't felt this happy for years. Tomorrow is Christmas Day! Let's have a party!"

And that's what they did.
Even the mayor was invited.
After that, Mervin made sure
that Zag and the children
never went hungry again.

Chapter 3

The man with a lump on his nose

Egbert had a lump on his nose. It had been there for five days. It just wouldn't go away.

"Go and see Mott the wizard," said his wife.

So Egbert went to find Mott. Mott looked hard at the lump, from many different angles.

Mott took out his book of spells. He hunted for the page about lumps.

"Do you want a cheap cure, or an expensive one?" he asked.

"Cheap, please!" said Egbert. "I only have one penny."

CURES FOR LUMPS AND SPOTS

1. **BEST CURE:**
Rub the lump with a piece of meat ....50p.

2. **SECOND BEST CURE:**
Rub the lump with a runner bean, Bury the bean 25p

3. **CHEAP CURE:**
Rub the lump with a stone. Put the stone in a paper bag. Bury the bag beside the nearest crossroads.....1p

WARNING!
The person who opens the bag will catch the lump.

Mott took the penny. He gave Egbert a stone, and told him what to do.

Egbert rubbed his nose with the stone. Then he put the stone  into a paper bag, and buried the bag near a crossroads.

Right away, Egbert's nose felt better. "Hurray!" he cried. "Three cheers for Mott!"

Egbert was thrilled. He went home and sat down with a book. He'd just reached an exciting part when his wife stormed in.

"Egbert!" she shouted. "Look what you've done!"

"But... I haven't done anything dear," Egbert said, in a small voice.

Come back here!

"Yes you have!" cried his wife. "I heard a man had buried a bag by the big tree. I thought it was treasure, so I dug it up. And now I have the lump!"

Chapter 4

The band of robbers

Pinchbeck the wizard and
Pogo the goblin were walking
together in the woods.

They were talking about a magic spell.

"The mushrooms must be picked at midnight," Pogo told Pinchbeck.

They were so busy talking, they didn't see a robber creeping up behind them.

Suddenly, the robber jumped
out. He hit Pinchbeck over
the head with his club.
"Give me your gold!"
he shouted.

Pinchbeck dropped the gold.
Pogo just ran.

The robber tied Pinchbeck
to a tree. Three hours later,
Pogo came back.

"My head hurts," groaned
Pinchbeck.

Slowly, Pinchbeck and Pogo climbed to the castle. They stopped in front of a huge wooden door and knocked.

Inside, the king and queen were having tea.

Was that a knock?

Who could it be?

"Who's there?" called the king.

"Pogo!" said Pogo. "With Pinchbeck the wizard."

"We were robbed in the woods. Please let us in."

"That's terrible!" said the king. "Come in at once."

The queen made some fresh tea, and wrapped Pinchbeck's head in bandages.

"The robbers came here too," she said.

"And they're coming back tomorrow," the king added. "If we don't give them two more bags of gold, they'll take over our castle."

And we don't have any gold left...

That night, Pinchbeck and Pogo stayed in the castle. They wished they could do something to help.

"My head's thumping too much," sighed Pinchbeck. "I can't think of any spells."

But Pogo had an idea. Early the next morning, he sneaked out of the castle.

He found two sacks in a shed and tiptoed through the garden.

If he tried hard enough, he might be able to work a spell. As fast as he could, he stuffed both sacks with leaves.

Then he hurried back to the castle.

When Pinchbeck saw the sacks, he clapped his hands with glee.

"Pogo! You've helped me to remember a spell!"

Umpi-grumpi,
do as you're told.
Fool those robbers and
turn into gold!

Yellow smoke filled the air, then...

Rat-a-tat-tat! The robbers were banging on the door.

"Open up!" they yelled. "We know you don't have any gold. The castle's ours!"

Oi, king! Out!

The queen began to cry.
"But we have nowhere to go,"
she sobbed.

"Tough!" said the robbers.

Just then, the robbers heard another voice. It was Pinchbeck.

The robbers couldn't believe their eyes. They blinked, and stared, then blinked again.

"Take your gold," said
Pinchbeck. "And make sure
we never see you here again."

"Ha! We're rich now," said
the chief robber. "Why would
we come back?"

And they set off. They rode
for five days and five nights.
The sacks were getting lighter
but the robbers didn't notice.
At last, they stopped to rest.

Tired and hungry, they decided to cheer themselves up. "Let's count our gold," they said.

"It's a trick!" shouted the chief robber. "We'll go back!" But it was no good. They'd come too far and were lost.

At the castle, Pinchbeck's head healed and his spells returned. It was time to go.

But before he left, he gave the king and queen a magic sack of gold which would never run out

Then he and Pogo headed back into the woods, the way they had come.

Try these other books in
Series One:

The Burglar's Breakfast: Alfie
Briggs is a burglar. After a hard
night of thieving, he likes to go home
to a tasty meal. But one day he gets
back to discover someone has
stolen his breakfast!

The Dinosaurs Next Door: Stan
loves living next door to Mr. Puff.
His house is full of amazing things.
Best of all are the dinosaur eggs –
until they begin to hatch...

The Monster Gang: Starting a
gang is a great idea. So is dressing
up like monsters. But if everyone
is in disguise, how do you know
who's who?

Series editor: Lesley Sims

Designed by
Katarina Dragoslavić

This edition first published in 2002 by Usborne Publishing Ltd.,
Usborne House, 83-85 Saffron Hill, London EC1N 8RT, England.
www.usborne.com
Copyright © 2002, 1980 Usborne Publishing Ltd.